This book belongs to:

....

....

....

Retold by Gaby Goldsack
Illustrated by Kim Blundell (John Martin & Artists)
Designed by Jester Designs

Language consultant: Betty Root

ISBN 1-84461-207-4

Marks and Spencer p.l.c.
PO Box 3339, Chester CH99 9QS
www.marksandspencer.com

Copyright © Exclusive Editions 2002

Printed in China

Chicken-Licken

Helping Your Child to Read

Learning to read is an exciting challenge for most children. From a very early age, sharing story books with children, talking about the pictures and guessing what might happen next are all very important parts of the reading experience.

Sharing reading

Set aside a regular quiet time to share reading with younger children, or to be on hand to encourage older children as they develop into independent readers.

First Readers are intended to encourage and support the early stages of learning to read. They present well-loved tales that children will happily listen to again and again. Familiarity helps children to identify some of the words and phrases.

When you feel your child is ready to move on a little, encourage them to join in so that you read the story aloud together. Always pause to talk about the pictures. The easy-to-read speech bubbles in **First Readers** provide an excellent 'joining-in' activity. The bright, clear illustrations and matching text will help children to understand the story.

Building confidence

In time, children will want to read *to* you. When this happens, be patient and give continual praise. They may not read all the words correctly, but children's substitutions are often very good guesses.

The repetition in each book is particularly helpful for building confidence. If your child cannot read a particular word, go back to the beginning of the sentence and read it together so the meaning is not lost. Most importantly, do not continue if your child is tired or simply in need of a change.

Reading alone

The next step is for your child to read alone. Try to be on hand to give help and support. Remember to give lots of encouragement and praise.

Together with other simple stories, **First Readers** will ensure that children will find reading an enjoyable and rewarding experience.

One day Chicken-Licken was in the field
when an acorn fell on her head.

"Oh dear!" said Chicken-Licken. "The
sky is falling in. I must tell the king."

So Chicken-Licken went off to tell the king. On the way, she met Cocky-Locky.

"Where are you going in such a hurry?" asked Cocky-Locky.

"The sky is falling in," said Chicken-Licken. "I'm going to tell the king."

"I'm coming with you," said Cocky-Locky.

On the way, Chicken-Licken and Cocky-Locky met Ducky-Lucky.

"Where are you going in such a hurry?" asked Ducky-Lucky.

Where are you going?

"The sky is falling in," said Chicken-Licken. "We are going to tell the king."

"I'm coming with you," said Ducky-Lucky.

On the way, Chicken-Licken, Cocky-Locky and Ducky-Lucky met Goosey-Loosey.

"Where are you going in such a hurry?" asked Goosey-Loosey.

"The sky is falling in," said Chicken-Licken. "We are going to tell the king."

"I'm coming with you," said Goosey-Loosey.

15

They all walked on until they met
Foxy-Loxy.

"Where are you going in such a hurry?" asked Foxy-Loxy.

"The sky is falling in," said Chicken-Licken. "We are going to tell the king."

"Ah," smiled Foxy-Loxy, who was a sly young fox. "You are going the wrong way. Follow me. I will show you the way.

So Chicken-Licken, Cocky-Locky, Ducky-Lucky and Goosey-Loosey followed Foxy-Loxy.

They walked on and on. At last, they came to a cave. "Follow me," said Foxy-Loxy. "This is a short cut."

But the cave was really
Foxy-Loxy's den.
Foxy-Loxy smiled as
Cocky-Locky, Ducky-Lucky
and Goosey-Loosey
followed her in.

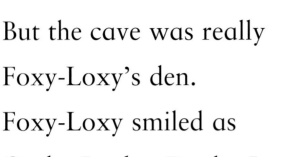

Chicken-Licken was about to follow
when Cocky-Locky cried out loud,
"Cock-a-doodle-doo!"

Cock-a-doodle-doo!

Chicken-Licken knew that something was wrong.

She turned and ran away.
She ran and ran.

Chicken-Licken did not stop until she got to the farmyard. Then she looked around for her friends.

Chicken-Licken waited and waited but her friends did not come back.

Chicken-Licken knew she was a
very lucky hen.

I'm a very lucky hen!

Chicken-Licken never did tell the king that the sky was falling in. But the sky never was falling in, was it?

Chicken-Licken was a very silly hen!

But she never went near a fox again.

Read and Say

How many of these words can you say?
The pictures will help you. Look back in
your book and see if you can find the
words in the story.

acorn

cave

Chicken-Licken

Cocky-Locky

Ducky-Lucky

field

Foxy-Loxy

Goosey-Loosey

hen

Titles in this series,
subject to availability:

Beauty and the Beast
Chicken-Licken
Cinderella
The Elves and the Shoemaker
The Emperor's New Clothes
The Enormous Turnip
The Gingerbread Man
Goldilocks and the Three Bears
Hansel and Gretel
Jack and the Beanstalk
Joseph's Coat of Many Colours
and Other Bible Stories
Little Red Riding Hood
Noah's Ark and Other Bible Stories
Rapunzel
Rumpelstiltskin
Sleeping Beauty
Snow White and the Seven Dwarfs
The Three Billy Goats Gruff
The Three Little Pigs
The Ugly Duckling